Penguin Readers

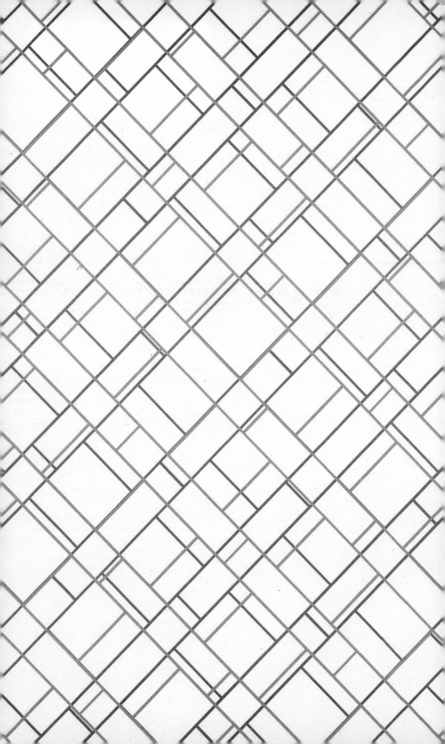

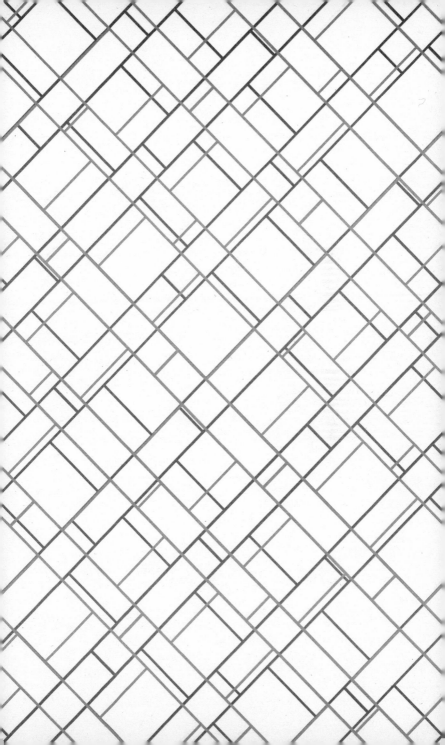

Penguin 🐧 Readers

LOKI AND THE GIANTS

BY ROGER LANCELYN GREEN

LEVEL

RETOLD BY KAREN KOVACS
ILLUSTRATED BY DYNAMO LTD
SERIES EDITOR: SORREL PITTS

PENGUIN BOOKS

UK | USA | Canada | Ireland | Australia
India | New Zealand | South Africa

Penguin Books is part of the Penguin Random House group of companies
whose addresses can be found at global.penguinrandomhouse.com.
www.penguin.co.uk www.puffin.co.uk www.ladybird.co.uk

Penguin
Random House
UK

Myths of the Norsemen first published as *The Saga of Asgard* by Puffin Books, 1960
Reprinted as *Myths of the Norsemen*, 1970
This Penguin Readers edition published by Penguin Books Ltd, 2020
001

Original text written by Roger Lancelyn Green
Text for Penguin Readers edition adapted by Karen Kovacs
Text copyright © Roger Lancelyn Green, 1960
Illustrated by Dynamo Ltd
Illustrations copyright © Penguin Books Ltd, 2020
Cover illustration © Studio Muti

The moral right of the original author has been asserted

Printed and bound in Great Britain by Clays Ltd, Elcograf S.p.A.

A CIP catalogue record for this book is available from the British Library

ISBN: 978-0-241-46338-3

All correspondence to:
Penguin Books
Penguin Random House Children's
One Embassy Gardens, 8 Viaduct Gardens,
London SW11 7BW

Contents

People in the story

Sten

Loki

Thor

Odin

Skrymsli

Freya

New words

chief

enemies

giant

god

goddess

hide

summer / winter

swan

wall

wheat

world

Before-reading questions

1 Read the back cover of the book. Write the correct answers in your notebook.
   a This is a *Viking* / **Roman** story.
   b Loki is **a giant** / **a god** / **a giant and a god.**
   c The gods and giants in this story **are** / **are not** friends.
   d Is Loki the gods' friend? – **Yes.** / **No.** / **The gods do not know.**

2 Look at the "People in the story" on pages 8–9. Write five questions in your notebook. For example, *Who has got long hair? Who is happy? Who is old?* Ask a friend your questions.

3 Sten and his friends live in Iceland. Find "Iceland" on this map.

4 Norway, Sweden and Denmark are Viking countries, too. Find them on the map.

Picture definitions of words in **bold** can be found on pages 10–11.

LOKI AND THE GIANTS

They're waiting for you.

Yes. The people here love my stories.

Sten, you're here! Let's go in.

The gods and giants are **enemies.**

Thor is a god. His father, Odin, is chief of the gods.

Loki is from Jotunheim. His father's a giant, but his mother's a **goddess**.

One morning, Thor and Odin are walking in Midgard. They meet a man there.

Help me!

Why?

The giant Skrymsli is coming to my house! My boy, Rogner, is his lunch!

I can't find the boy.

Skrymsli goes home.

But in the morning . . .

Skrymsli is coming to my house. Rogner is his lunch!

Thor, can you help Rogner?

Yes. I can hide him.

Thor, help Rogner!

I can't find the boy.

Skrymsli goes home.

29

But in the morning . . .

Skrymsli is coming to my house. Rogner is his lunch!

Father, who's that?

It's Loki. He can help Rogner.

But Loki is from Jotunheim. Is he our friend or our enemy? We don't know.

Hide in this fish egg.

Loki, help Rogner!

Loki is from Jotunheim, but he helps the gods.

One day, in Asgard . . .

Asgard doesn't have a **wall**. The giants can come in.

The man and his horse work every day.

During-reading questions

Write the answers to these questions in your notebook.

1 Which country do Sten and his friends live in?
2 What is Sten's work?
3 Who lives in Asgard?
4 Who lives in Midgard?
5 Who lives in Jotunheim?

1 Who is Thor's father?
2 Who is Loki's father?
3 Who is Loki's mother?

1 Does Odin like Loki?
2 Does Thor like Loki?
3 Does Skrymsli eat Rogner?
4 Who kills Skrymsli?

1 Why do the gods want a wall for Asgard?
2 A man can make the wall. He does not want money.
   What does he want?
3 The man does not make the wall in one winter. Why not?

After-reading questions

1 Where does Rogner hide? (There are three places.)

2 Who helps Rogner? (There are three people.)

3 Thor says on page 46: "[Loki]'s with the giants, I think."
   Is Thor right?

4 Who is your favourite person in the story?

5 Do you like Loki?

6 Is Loki good or bad, do you think?

Exercises

1 Look at the picture. Complete these sentences in your notebook, using the words from the box.

Asgard	People	Midgard	The gods
	Jotunheim	The giants	

1 World one is .....*Asgard*..... .....*The gods*.... live there.

2 World two is .... live there.

3 World three is .... live there.

2 **Make these sentences negative in your notebook.**

1 The gods and the giants are friends.
The gods and the giants are not friends.

2 Thor is chief of the gods.

3 Thor likes Loki.

4 The giants help people.

5 People can kill the giants.

6 Skrymsli eats Rogner.

3 **Put these sentences in the correct order in your notebook.**

a .... Thor and Odin meet a man in Midgard. Skrymsli is coming!

b .... Loki kills Skrymsli.

c .... Thor hides Rogner in a swan.

d .... Loki hides Rogner in a fish egg.

e ...*1*.... Sten tells the story of Loki.

f .... Odin hides Rogner in some wheat.

g .... Rogner stands on the beach.

4 **Complete these sentences in your notebook with words from pages 10–11.**

1 Thor's father is a ....*god*........, but Loki's father is a ....*giant*........

2 Odin .... Rogner in the ....

3 A .... is a bird.

4 Freya is a ....

5 In the .... it is hot, and in the .... it is cold.

5 **Look at the first picture on page 42, and answer the questions in your notebook.**

1 Who is in the picture?
   A man, Loki, Odin, Thor and Freya.

2 What is Loki doing?

3 What are the gods doing?

4 What is Thor thinking, do you think?

6 In your notebook, put these words in the correct group.

> Odin   Asgard   Sleipnir   Jotunheim   Thor
> Freya   Skrymsli   Midgard   Svadilfari

Example:

gods/goddesses	giants	horses	worlds
Odin			

7 Complete these sentences in your notebook with the present simple or the present continuous.

1 Where ...*do*... people ...*live*... (live)? – They ...*live*... (live) in Midgard.

2 Thor .... (not like) Loki.

3 Help me! Skrymsli .... (come) to my house!

4 Asgard .... (not have) a wall.

5 What .... that man .... (do)? – Can't you see? He .... (make) a wall.

6 What .... the man .... (want)? – He .... (want) Freya.

8 Complete these sentences in your notebook, using the words from the box.

listen	tomorrow	Jotunheim	sun
moon	Sleipnir	evening	Freya

1 The people ....*listen*........... to Sten's stories.
2 "Good ...., Chief."
3 The third world is ....
4 The man wants the goddess ....
5 The man wants the ....
6 And he wants the ....
7 "Summer starts .... Look at the wall!"
8 Svadilfari and the white horse have a child. Its name is ....

9 Write the correct word. Then, answer the question in your notebook.

1 The man makes the wall. How **much** / **many** time does he have? *He has one winter.*
2 How **much** / **many** money does the man want?
3 How **much** / **many** horses are there in the story?

58

Project work

1 You are speaking to your friend on the phone. You are watching Skrymsli, Rogner and the gods. What do you see? Tell your friend.

Example: Oh no! Skrymsli is coming. But it's OK. Odin is helping Rogner. He . . .

2 Choose some pages from the story. Act them out with your friends. For example, you are Loki, one friend is the man and one friend is Freya. Say the words from the story.

3 Write a new ending for the story.

4 Make a poster about the Viking gods, the Viking giants or the Viking worlds.
   - What do you know about them? Write it on the poster.
   - What do they look like? Draw pictures, or find pictures on the internet.

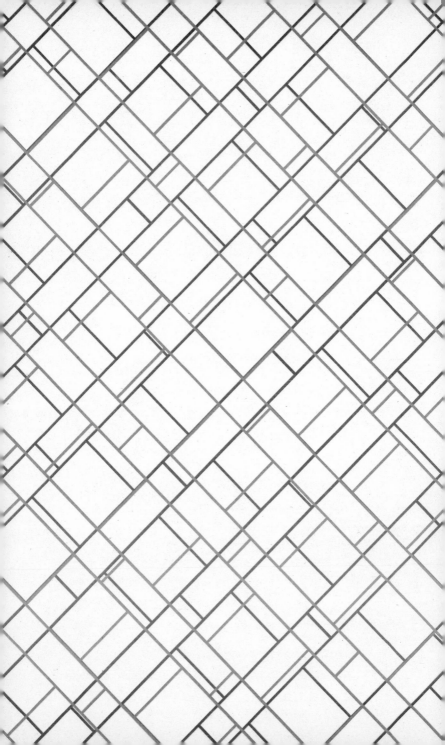

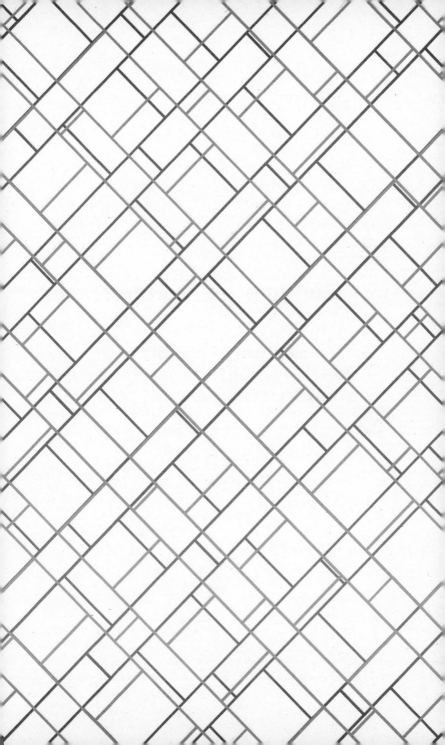

Penguin  Readers

Visit **www.penguinreaders.co.uk**
for FREE Penguin Readers resources
and digital and audio versions of this book.